CHILDREN'S
STORYTIME COLLECTION

Ursula's Umbrella

AND OTHER STORIES

Contents

Ursula's Umbrella

Ursula was a little girl who longed for adventure. She loved reading stories about far-away places and explorers, and even children like herself who had amazing adventures. "Why doesn't anything interesting ever happen to me?" she sighed. "How I wish I could fly to the moon or dive to the deepest part of the ocean. What fun it would be!"

One windy day, Ursula went out for a walk. She took her umbrella with her because it looked as though it might be going to rain. Ursula's umbrella was red with a shiny black handle. It was also very large indeed. People used to laugh as Ursula walked along the street with her umbrella up. It looked so big and Ursula was so small that it seemed as though the umbrella was walking along all by itself!

As Ursula walked up the street she felt a few raindrops on her nose. "Better put up my umbrella," she thought. She unfurled her umbrella and lifted it up above her head. As she did so, a great gust of wind came and swept her right off the pavement. It carried her past the upstairs windows of the houses, past the roofs and the chimney pots and up, up, into the sky. Ursula clung tightly to the umbrella handle. She was surprised to find she didn't feel the least bit frightened. No, not a bit. She felt very excited. She looked down and saw streets and factories whizzing past far below. Then she saw fields and something that looked like a silver thread snaking through the countryside. "A river!" thought Ursula.

Now she could see the coastline, and soon the umbrella was carrying her out over the ocean. At first when she looked down the sea was grey, but gradually it turned to the deepest blue with frothy white waves. "How I'd love a swim," thought Ursula. At that moment she felt the umbrella starting to descend. Looking down she could see that they were heading for an island in the middle of the ocean. Soon she was floating past the tops of palm trees and, as she touched the ground, she felt sand under her feet.

"I'm going for a swim!" said Ursula to herself. She folded up her umbrella and set off to the beach. The water felt deliciously warm as Ursula paddled about. She looked down and saw that the water was amazingly clear. She could see brightly coloured fish darting in and out of the coral. "Wow!" exclaimed Ursula out loud and then "Wow!" again, though this time much louder as she looked up and saw a black fin skimming through the water towards her. "Shark!" she shrieked, but no-one heard.

Then all of a sudden a gust of wind made her umbrella unfurl itself and float towards her in the water, like a boat. Ursula made a dash for the umbrella, hurled herself into it and floated away across the sea. "That was quite an adventure!" she thought.

After a while, Ursula looked out over the rim of the umbrella and saw that it was heading for the shore again. This time, when Ursula stepped out of the umbrella, she found that she was at the edge of a jungle. Folding up the umbrella, she set off into the forest. She followed an overgrown path through the trees. "I wonder where this leads?" thought Ursula. She wiped her brow and swatted the insects that flew in front of her face. Deeper and deeper into the jungle she went.

Suddenly she heard the sound of rushing water and found herself standing on the banks of a river. All at once she heard another sound. It was the crashing noise of some enormous beast approaching through the trees.

5

Where could she run to? Suddenly she felt the umbrella being blown from her hand. To her amazement it fell to the ground, stretching right across the river like a bridge. Ursula walked over to the other side, not daring to look down at the torrent below. When she was safely on the far bank she looked back to see a large puma, with glittering green eyes, glaring at her from the opposite bank. "That was a lucky escape!" thought Ursula.

Ursula could see a mountain through the trees and decided to head towards it. "I'll be able to get a good view from the top and maybe find my way home," she thought. She struggled on through the forest and eventually found herself at the foot of the mountain. There seemed to be no way up the sheer rock face.

Ursula was on the point of despair when suddenly another great gust of wind blew up. It carried Ursula, clinging to her opened umbrella, all the way up to the top of the mountain.

At the top of the mountain, the umbrella let her gently down again and her feet landed in deep snow. By now it was blowing a blizzard and she could not see anything except white snowflakes in all directions. "There's only one thing to do," thought Ursula. She put the umbrella on the snow, sat on it and whizzed all the way down the other side of the mountain.

When she reached the bottom, to her surprise, the umbrella sledge didn't stop but carried on through the snowstorm until eventually, after a very long time, it came to a halt right outside her own front door. "Well, that was quite an adventure," said Ursula, shaking the snow off the umbrella, before folding it up.

She stepped inside the front door. "Wherever have you been?" said her mother. "You look as though you've been to the ends of the Earth and back."

"Well I have," Ursula was about to say. But then she thought that no-one would believe her and it was nicer to keep her adventures to herself. And that is what she did.

The Singing Bear

Long ago, there lived a young boy named Peter. He was a gentle lad who loved all creatures, but most of all he loved the animals and birds of the forest. Many a time he had mended a jay's broken wing, or set a badger free from a cruel trap.

One day, the fair came to town and Peter was very excited. He could see brightly coloured tents being put up in the field and carts arriving with mysterious looking loads. As soon as the fair was open Peter was off with his penny in his pocket to try his luck. First of all he had a go at the coconut shy. Then he tried to climb the greasy pole. Finally, he used his last farthing on the tombola stall. He was about to head for home when out of the corner of his eye he caught a glimpse of a dreadful sight. Lying in a cage, looking sad and forlorn, was a large brown bear. On a small plate at the front of the cage was the bear's name: Lombard. He looked so dejected that Peter immediately vowed to set him free. The cage was strongly padlocked and Peter knew not how he could break the lock. He turned to make his way home, with the bear gazing pitifully after him.

That night, Peter tossed and turned in his bed. What was he to do? He wasn't strong enough to break into the bear's cage and his keeper would surely not agree to set him free. In the middle of the night, he resolved to return to the fairground to comfort the bear.

He slipped out of bed and made his way by the light of the moon back to the fairground. To his astonishment he found the bear singing a song to himself in a beautiful voice. For a while Peter listened to the lovely sound of the bear's singing. Then he had an idea. He remembered a piece of paper he had seen pinned to the palace gate.

"Don't cry, Lombard," he said. "I think I know a way to get you out of here. But first you must teach me your song." The bear was happy to oblige and soon the two of them were singing the song together. Then Peter said, "I must go, but I'll be back tomorrow. And remember, when you see me, be ready to sing your song."

The next day, Peter put on his very best clothes and set off for the palace. Pinned to the gate was the piece of paper, just as Peter had remembered. On the paper was written in a handsome script: *The King Requires a Minstrel with a Fine Voice. Apply Within.*

Peter knocked at the gate. He was shown into a beautiful golden gallery where a row of minstrels were waiting to be auditioned. A courtier rang a little bell for silence, and in came the king. He sat down at his great gold throne.

"Let the audition begin," cried the king. The first minstrel stepped forward. He sang a song in a sweet, high voice that tugged at the heart and reduced the court to tears. The next minstrel sang in a deep, rich voice that sent shivers down the spine, so that the birds in the trees stopped singing to listen. The next minstrel sang a song that was so witty and amusing that the entire court wept with laughter.

At last it was Peter's turn. He stepped forward, gave a deep bow and said, "I beg your majesty's permission to perform my song out of doors, so that all the wild creatures of the forest might hear it, too."

"What a strange request!" said the king. However, if the truth be told, he had grown quite sleepy listening to so many beautiful songs and thought the fresh air might liven him up. "Very well, but it had better be worth it!" he said, giving Peter a fierce look.

"Follow me!" called Peter. He led the king, the court and all the minstrels out of the palace gates and down the road.

"Where are we going?" and "This is very untoward," they muttered. At last they reached the fairground, but Peter didn't stop until he was in view of Lombard's cage. Lombard saw him and Peter winked at the bear.

"This is where I'd like to sing for you," said Peter to the king.

The king's royal eyebrows rose higher and higher as he looked around him. "Well, I must say this is very odd indeed! However, as we've come this far, we may as well hear your song. Proceed!" said the king.

Peter opened his mouth and mimed the words while Lombard sang. It was the most beautiful song that anyone had ever heard. By the end of the song, the king was sobbing tears of joy, mirth and sorrow all together.

"That was the finest song I ever heard,"
he said. "You have won the audition
and I would like you to be my minstrel."

Peter took another low bow. "Sire,"
he said. "Would that I could accept,
but in all honesty it was not I who
sang but my friend, Lombard the bear."
Everyone gasped as they saw the bear in his cage.

For a moment the king looked furious. But then he began to
smile and said, "I praise you for your honesty, Peter, and I would
very much like to have Lombard for my minstrel. Chancellor, bring
me the royal purse."

The king paid Lombard's keeper handsomely, who was then
delighted to set the bear free. Lombard became the king's minstrel
and was famous throughout the land, and from then on Peter went
to the palace each day and sang duets with his friend, the bear.
And it is said that, in the end, Peter married the king's daughter.

The King Who Ate Too Much

Long ago, in a kingdom far, far away, there lived a greedy king. Now the thing that this king loved, more than anything else in the whole world, was food. He simply couldn't get enough of it. Ever since he was a little prince, he had been allowed to eat whatever he wanted, whenever he wanted it. And because he was always eating, he just got fatter and fatter and fatter with every day that passed.

When he became king, his appetite seemed to get even bigger! As soon as he woke in the morning, he would have his servants bring him an enormous breakfast. After eating several huge, steaming bowls of porridge, he would eat slice after slice of hot, buttered toast and jam, followed by all the boiled eggs that the royal chickens could lay.

In case he got a little hungry mid-morning, he would have a snack – usually ten or more chocolate cakes, washed down with as many cups of tea!

At lunchtime, the table would groan with the weight of all the pies, sandwiches, fruit and biscuits that the greedy king was about to gobble down.

For afternoon tea, it would be cakes, cakes and more cakes.

But the king's biggest meal was supper! The royal cooks toiled for most of the day to prepare this feast. When it was time for the king to eat, one servant after another would carry in great bowls of steaming soup, plates of fish of every kind, followed by huge roasts and dishes of vegetables. Down it all went, followed by fruit and jelly. At last, the king would be full and he would retire to his bed for the night.

But the king's greedy eating habits also made him a very thoughtless king. No-one dared tell him that much of the wealth of the kingdom had to be spent on his huge meals. In the meantime, his loyal subjects were going hungry and becoming poor and needy.

One day, just after the king had eaten his usual big lunch, he began to feel very strange. Not only did he feel even bigger than usual, he also began to feel very light. Suddenly, without any warning, he started floating up from the table and into the air like a big balloon.

"Help! Get me down!" he cried.

16

The royal courtiers and servants jumped up and down and tried in vain to grab the king as he floated upwards, but in no time at all he had floated out of reach. Before anyone knew it, he had floated out of the castle window. Out across the royal grounds he went, over the river and towards the woods and mountains of his kingdom.

"Wooaa-aaah!" cried the king, as he disappeared from view.

Soon, the king began to float over a small farm. He looked down and saw the farmer's children, dressed only in rags, searching for firewood. Some thin, hungry cows stood nearby chewing on a few meagre pieces of hay.

Over the next farm he floated, and a similar sad scene met his gaze. Dressed in rags, a poor farmer and his family toiled their soil hoping to grow enough to eat.

Next he floated over a small village. Everywhere he looked he saw shabby, run-down houses in need of repair and people in the streets begging for money.

Every farm and every village the king floated over told the same story of hunger and misery. The king suddenly felt very sad and very ashamed. He had been so busy enjoying himself eating that he hadn't given a thought to the plight of his subjects. While he was getting fatter and fatter, they were all getting thinner and poorer.

Now, a gust of wind was blowing the king back towards his castle. As he was passing over the castle, he suddenly felt himself falling. Down, down, he went until he landed back into the castle grounds with a great thud and a bounce.

That very day, the king sent out a royal proclamation. All his loyal subjects were to come to the castle for a huge feast, after which they would all be given a purse full of gold.

As for the king, he was never greedy again. Instead of spending all his money on food for himself, he gave enough to all the people in the land so that they would never be hungry or poor again.

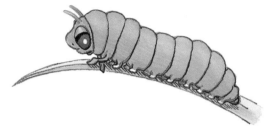

The Jealous Caterpillar

One spring day a green caterpillar sat on a leaf. He watched a beautiful butterfly flutter past him on the breeze. "It's not fair. Here I am stuck on this boring leaf with nothing to do and nowhere to go while that lucky creature can fly across the world and see far-off lands," thought the caterpillar crossly. "And what's more," he continued to himself, "not only has that butterfly got wings with which to fly, but he's beautiful, too. Look at poor me. I'm just a dull green. No-one will notice me because I'm the same colour as the leaf." The caterpillar really did feel very sorry for himself, and rather jealous. "Go and enjoy yourself. Don't worry about me," he called spitefully to the butterfly.

But the butterfly hadn't heard a single word the caterpillar had been muttering, and soon he flew away. The caterpillar suddenly decided that he was going to be like the butterfly. "I'll learn how to fly and I'll paint myself lovely colours so that I look beautiful, too," he thought. He looked around for something to paint himself with but, of course, there was nothing at all on the leaf. Then he tried to fly. He launched himself from his leaf and tried to flap his tail, but all he did was land on the leaf below.

Along came a ladybird. "Aha!" thought the caterpillar. "Here's a beautiful creature who knows how to fly. I'll ask her to teach me." So the caterpillar said, "Hello, I've been admiring your beautiful wingcase. Could you tell me how I, too, could be beautiful? And can you teach me to fly?"

The ladybird looked at the caterpillar. "Be patient and wait a while," she said wisely, "and soon enough you'll get what you want." And with that the ladybird went on her way.

21

"Whatever can she mean? She's just too proud to teach me," the caterpillar thought jealously.

Some time later a bee buzzed past and landed on a nearby leaf. "Aha!" thought the caterpillar. "Here's a beautiful creature who knows how to fly. I'll ask him to teach me." So the caterpillar said, "Hello, I've been admiring your beautiful striped back. Could you tell me how I, too, could be beautiful? And can you teach me to fly?"

The bee looked at the caterpillar. "You'll find out soon enough, young man," said the bee sternly. And with that he went on his way.

"Whatever can he mean? He's just too haughty to teach me," the caterpillar thought jealously.

Now a while later along came a bird. "Aha!" thought the caterpillar once more. "Here's a beautiful creature who knows how to fly. I'll ask him to teach me." So once again the caterpillar said, "Hello, I've been admiring your beautiful feathers. Could you tell me how I, too, could be beautiful? And can you teach me to fly?"

The bird looked at the caterpillar and thought to himself slyly that here was a very silly caterpillar, but he would make a tasty snack for his chicks. "Let's see if I can trick him," he thought.

"I can't give you wings and I can't make you beautiful. But I can show you the world. I expect you'd like to see the world, wouldn't you, little caterpillar?" said the bird.

"Oh, yes!" said the caterpillar in great excitement.

"Climb upon my back then, little caterpillar!" said the crafty bird.

The caterpillar did as he was told and the bird flew off towards his nest. At first the caterpillar clung tightly to the bird's back but soon he felt quite sleepy and eventually he dozed off and slipped from the bird's back. Down he fell through the air and landed on a leaf, but still he didn't wake up. Soon he was wrapped in a soft, brown, papery cocoon from which he would not wake up for a long while.

Meanwhile, the bird reached his nest. "Look at the treat I've brought you," he said to his chicks.

They looked very puzzled. "What treat, Dad?" one of them piped up.

"This nice juicy caterpillar," said the bird, shaking the feathers on his back. "Climb down, little caterpillar," he said. But of course there was nothing there. Now it was the father's turn to look puzzled, while the chicks laughed at him.

24

"Well, I must have dropped him," he said. "I've never done that before," he added. He flew out of the nest in search of the caterpillar but he was nowhere to be seen. Once he saw a strange brown, papery parcel on a leaf, but in the end the bird had to return to the nest with his beak empty.

A long while later the caterpillar woke up. "I must get out of this stuffy wrapping," he thought, as he pushed his way out. He stood on the leaf and yawned and stretched. As he stretched, he noticed to his amazement two pairs of beautiful wings spreading out on either side of his body. "Are they really mine?" he wondered. He tried lifting and turning them and yes, he could make them work. He looked at his reflection in a raindrop and saw a lovely butterfly staring back at him. "So the ladybird and the bee were right," he exclaimed. "How foolish I was to be a jealous caterpillar," he declared to a passing ant, "for now I am a beautiful butterfly after all."

Rapunzel

There once lived a man and his wife who had long wished for a child. At last their wish was granted and the wife found that she was expecting a baby. At the back of their house was a garden that was filled with the most beautiful flowers and herbs. However, the man and his wife did not dare enter the garden, for it was owned by a wicked witch, of whom everyone was scared.

One day, when the woman was standing by her window looking down into the garden, she saw a flower bed full of the prettiest Rapunzel plants she had ever seen. They looked so fresh and green that she felt a great craving to eat some of them. Day after day she would sit by her window, staring at the Rapunzel plants for hours on end. Eventually she became quite pale and miserable.

"What's wrong, my dear?" said her husband.

"I must have some of that Rapunzel," she replied, "or I may die."

The poor husband decided that the only thing to do was to steal into the witch's garden at night and take some of the plants. Late one night the man climbed the high wall that surrounded the garden and hastily snatched a bunch of Rapunzel plants and made off with them.

His wife was delighted. She made a salad of them that was so delicious that the next day she said to her husband, "I must have more of that delicious Rapunzel."

So that night the husband stole once more into the witch's garden. Imagine his horror when he dropped on to the grass to find the witch there lying in wait for him. "How dare you come into my garden and steal my Rapunzel plants," she shrieked. "You'll live to regret this."

"Please have mercy on me," begged the man. "I'm not really a thief. I came to help my wife, who is expecting our first child. She told me she would die if she didn't have some of your Rapunzel to eat."

Then the witch changed her tune. "By all means," she said, "take as much as you like. But in exchange you must give me the baby when it is born. Don't worry – I will care for it as if I were its mother. What do you say?" The man was so terrified that he hastily agreed to what the witch had said. When his wife gave birth to a baby girl the witch immediately appeared to take the child. The witch named her Rapunzel, after the plants that had caused all the trouble, and took the child away with her.

Rapunzel grew very beautiful, strong and healthy, with long golden hair that fell past her waist. When she was twelve years old the witch locked her away at the top of a tower in the middle of a forest. The tower had neither stairs nor a door, but only one window at the top so that nobody but the witch could reach her.

Each day when the witch visited her, she would stand below the girl's window and call out, "Rapunzel, Rapunzel, let down your hair, that I may climb without a stair."

Then the girl would wind her long tresses around the window hook and lower her hair all the way to the ground. The witch would climb up it as if it were a ladder. In this way, Rapunzel's lonely life went on for several years.

One day, a young prince was riding in the forest when he heard a sweet voice. It was Rapunzel singing to herself. The prince was so entranced that he followed the sound and came upon the tower.

But when he could find no way in he became discouraged
and rode home. Rapunzel's lovely voice had stirred his heart so
deeply, however, that he returned day after day to hear her
singing.

One day, as he stood behind a tree, he saw the witch appear
and heard her calling, "Rapunzel, Rapunzel, let down your hair,
that I may climb without a stair."

Then he saw a mass of golden hair tumble down and watched
the witch climb up it to the window. "Is that the way up?"
thought the prince. "Then I will climb the golden ladder, too."

The next day, around dusk, the prince went to the tower and
called, "Rapunzel, Rapunzel, let down your hair, that I may climb
without a stair."

Immediately the tresses fell down and the prince climbed up.
At first sight of the prince, Rapunzel was afraid, but the prince
addressed her in such a friendly way that she knew she could trust
him. "Once I had heard your voice," said the prince, "I couldn't rest
until I saw you. Now I cannot rest until you agree to marry me."

Rapunzel by now had fallen truly in love with the young man,
so she willingly accepted. "I wish I could come away with you," said
Rapunzel. "You must bring some silk with you each time you visit,
and I shall weave a ladder of silk and then I will be able to escape."

Each day the witch visited Rapunzel and each night the
prince came. The witch suspected nothing until one day
Rapunzel forgot herself and said to the witch, "Why are you so
much heavier to pull up than the prince?"

"Oh, treacherous girl," screamed the witch. "You have deceived me!" She snatched up a pair of scissors and cut off all Rapunzel's lovely hair. Then the witch drove Rapunzel from the tower and left her in a wild and desolate place to fend for herself as best she could.

That night, along came the prince to the tower and said, as usual, "Rapunzel, Rapunzel, let down your hair, that I may climb without a stair."

But the witch was lying in wait. She tied Rapunzel's hair to the window hook and let the golden tresses fall to the ground. Up climbed the prince full of joy, as always. But when he stepped in through the window, it was not his beautiful Rapunzel that met his gaze but the icy glare of the witch. "Aha!" cried the witch with a sneer. "So you thought you could steal my girl, did you? Well she's gone and you'll never set eyes on her again."

Beside himself with grief, the prince threw himself from the tower and would have died had he not landed in the thickest briars. Although he survived, the thorns pierced his eyes and blinded him. For many years he wandered through the wilderness grieving for his lost Rapunzel and living on whatever he could find to eat. Eventually, he wandered into the same part of the wilderness where Rapunzel lived in miserable poverty with the twins she had borne.

Just as he had done so many years ago, the prince heard a sweet voice coming through the trees. He made his way towards the sound of the voice. Suddenly Rapunzel saw him and straight away she recognised him. She ran to him and threw her arms around him weeping. As she wept tears of joy and sorrow, two teardrops fell into his eyes, healing them and restoring his sight.

Then the two were united again and the prince took Rapunzel and their children back to his own kingdom, and they all lived happily ever after.

The Greedy Hamster

There was once a hamster named Harry. He was a very greedy hamster. As soon as his food was put in his cage he gobbled it all up, and then he would push his little nose through the bars in the hope that something else to eat might come within reach. From his cage he could see all manner of delicious food on the kitchen table – and the smells! The scent of freshly baked bread was enough to send him spinning round in his exercise wheel with frustration.

"It's not fair!" he grumbled to himself. "They're all eating themselves silly out there and here am I simply starving to death!" (At this point he would usually remember the large meal he had just eaten and that his tummy was indeed still rather full.)

"If only I could get out of this beastly cage, I could feast on all the food I deserve," he announced to himself, and the thought of all those tasty morsels made his mouth water.

One night after the family had gone to bed, Harry was having one last spin in his wheel before retiring to his sawdust mattress. As he spun around, he heard an unfamiliar squeaky noise.

"That's funny," thought Harry. "The little girl oiled my wheel only today. It surely can't need oiling again." He stopped running and got off the wheel, but the squeak continued. Harry sat quite still on his haunches and listened intently. Then he realised it was the door to his cage squeaking. The door! The door was flapping open. The little girl had not closed it properly before she went to bed. Harry did a little dance of glee. Then he went to the door and looked cautiously out in case there was any danger. But all seemed to be well. The cat was asleep on a chair. The dog was sleeping soundly on the floor.

Now, as well as being a greedy hamster, Harry was also clever. Once outside the cage, the first thing he did was look at the catch to see how it worked. Yes! He was pretty sure he could work out how to open it from the inside now. Harry sniffed the air. There were some tasty titbits left over from a birthday party on the table. He could smell the sugar icing, and soon he was on the table, cramming his mouth with odds and ends of cheese sandwiches and pieces of chocolate cake. When he had eaten his fill, he stuffed his cheek pouches with ginger biscuits and ran back into his cage, closing the door behind him.

"Good!" thought Harry. "Now I will never be hungry again."

The next night Harry let himself out of his cage and helped himself to food, and again the next night and the night after that. He feasted on everything and anything – nuts, bananas, pieces of bread, left-over jelly and slices of pizza were all pushed into his greedy mouth. Each time he returned to his cage he filled his cheeks with more and more food. He did not notice that he was getting fatter and fatter, although he was aware that he could no longer run round in his wheel without falling off! Then one night, he undid the door catch but found he was simply too wide to get through the door!

For a while Harry sat in a very bad temper in the corner of the cage. His cheeks were still bulging with food from his last midnight feast, but the greedy hamster wanted more. Then he had an idea. "I'll get that lazy cat to help," he thought. He squealed at the top of his voice until the cat, who had been dreaming of rats, woke up with a start.

"What do you want?" she hissed at Harry. Harry explained his problem.

"Of course, I'd be only too pleased to help," said the crafty cat, thinking to herself here was an extra dinner! With her strong claws she bent back the door frame of the cage, until there was just enough room for Harry to squeeze through. Then, with a mighty swipe of her paw, she caught him and gobbled him whole. She felt extremely full, what with Harry and all his food inside her. She could barely crawl back to her chair and soon she was fast asleep again and snoring loudly with her mouth open. Inside her tummy Harry, too, felt very uncomfortable. Every time the cat snored, it sounded like a thunderstorm raging around his head.

"I must get out of here," he thought, and headed for the cat's open jaws. But he was far too fat to get out again. Then he had another idea. Through the cat's jaws he could see the dog lying on the floor.

"Help! Help!" he squeaked. The dog woke up to a very strange sight. There was the cat lying on the chair snoring, but she also seemed to be squeaking, "Help!" The dog put his head on one side. He was very perplexed. Then he saw a pair of beady eyes and some fine whiskers inside the cat's mouth. It was Harry!

"Get me out of here, please," pleaded Harry.

Now the dog did not very much like the cat, so he was quite willing to help the hamster.

"I'll stick my tail in the cat's mouth. Then you hang on while I pull you out," said the dog. "But mind you don't make a sound and wake the cat, or she'll surely bite my tail!" The dog gingerly put the tip of his tail inside the cat's open jaws, just far enough for Harry's little paws to grab hold. Then he pulled with all his might. Out popped Harry and out of Harry popped all the food he'd stored in his cheeks – peanuts, an apple core and a slice of jam tart!

"Thank you, thank you," gasped Harry as he made a dash for his cage and slammed the door shut. "I think I'll stay in my cage from now on and just stick to the food I'm given!"

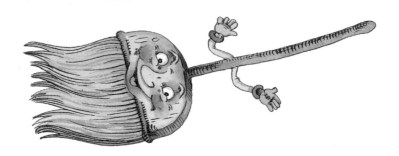

The Naughty Broom

"Goodness me, what a lot of dirt and dust there is all over this kitchen floor," said the maid. She was a very house-proud maid, and didn't like dirt and dust on her floor one little bit. Out came the broom from its place in the cupboard in the corner, and soon the maid was busily sweeping the floor and brushing all the dirt and dust into a big dustpan.

Unfortunately, this kitchen also had elves living in it. They were too tiny to see, of course, but if you upset them they could be very mischievous indeed. As the broom worked away, it swept into one dark corner where the elves were having a party. Suddenly the king elf was swept away from their little table and into the dustpan! The next thing he knew he was being thrown, with all the other rubbish, on to the rubbish tip.

Coughing and spluttering with rage, the king elf finally climbed out from under all the rubbish in the rubbish tip and stood on top of it. He picked the dirt and dust out of his ears and nose, pulled a fish bone from out of his trousers and tried to look as king-like as he could, having just been thrown on to a rubbish tip. "Who did this?" he squeaked at the top of his voice. "I'll make someone very, very sorry indeed," he vowed.

Eventually he made his way back to the house, and into the kitchen again. The other elves looked at the king elf and did their best not to laugh. For the king elf was still looking very dirty and untidy, and still had bits of rubbish stuck all over him. But the other elves knew better than to laugh at the king, because he was likely to cast a bad spell on them if they did.

"It was the broom that did it," chorused all the other elves.

"Right," said the king elf, "then I'm going to cast a bad spell on the broom."

The broom was by now back in its cupboard. The king elf marched over to the cupboard and jumped in through the keyhole. The king elf pointed to the broom and said,

"Bubble, bubble, gubble, gubble,

Go and cause a lot of trouble!"

And with that the broom suddenly stood to attention, its bristles quivering. It was night time now and everyone in the house was asleep. The broom opened its cupboard door and sprang into the kitchen. It then unlocked the kitchen door and went outside. Straight to the rubbish tip it went, and with a flick of its bristles, swept a huge pile of rubbish back into the kitchen. Tin cans, dirt, dust, chicken bones and goodness knows what else all got swept on to the kitchen floor. The broom then closed the kitchen door, took itself back to its cupboard and all was quiet until morning.

42

When the maid came down into the kitchen, she couldn't
believe her eyes. "Who has made this awful mess?" she said. "If I
find out it was those cats . . ." she threatened. She took the broom
from the cupboard and swept all the rubbish back outside again.

The next night, the same thing happened. Once it was quiet
and everyone in the house was asleep, out of its cupboard came
the broom, and into the house came all the rubbish again, swept
there as before by the naughty broom. This time, there were fish
heads, old bottles and all the soot from the fireplaces.

Well, the maid was speechless. After clearing up again, she
got the gardener to burn all the rubbish from the rubbish tip, so
that nothing else could be brought in – although she still had no
idea how it had happened.

That very night, the naughty broom decided it would make a
mess in a different way. So instead of sweeping in rubbish from
outside, the broom flew up to the shelves and knocked all the
jars to the ground. With a crash they fell to the floor, one after
another, and spread their contents everywhere.

"Stop this AT ONCE!" demanded a voice suddenly.

The broom stopped its mischief.

"What do you think you are doing?" said the voice again. The
voice had come from a very stern-looking fairy who was now
standing on the draining board, with her hands on her hips.
What the broom did not know was that one of the bottles it had
knocked down contained a good fairy, imprisoned by the elves.
Now she was at last free, the spell was broken and it was her turn
to cast a spell.

"Broom, broom, sweep this floor,
Make it cleaner than ever before.
Find the elves that cast your spell,
And sweep them off into the well," she chanted.

The broom went to work. It seemed to sweep so fast that its bristles just became a blur. Into this corner it went, then into that, and into every nook and cranny it swept. Every bit of dirt and dust, and all the broken bottles, were swept into the dustpan and then out of the house. Then it came back and swept all the elves down into the well where they couldn't do any more mischief.

In the morning, the maid came down to find a spotlessly clean kitchen. She was puzzled to find some of the jars missing, but between you and me she was also rather pleased. It just meant that there were fewer things to dust.

This is a Parragon Book
This edition published in 2000

Parragon
Queen Street House
4 Queen Street
Bath BA1 1HE

Written by Derek Hall, Alison Morris and
Louisa Somerville
Illustrated by Jeremy Bays, Natalie Bould,
Maureen Galvani, Martin Orme, Sara Silcock
and Kirsty Wilson

Printed and bound in Spain
ISBN 0-75253-535-8